Apple Farmer Annie

BY MONICA WELLINGTON

PUFFIN BOOKS

PUFFIN BOOKS
Published by Penguin Group
Penguin Young Readers Group,
345 Hudson Street, New York, New York 10014, U.S.A.
Penguin Books Ltd, 80 Strand, London WC2R ORL, England
Penguin Books Canada Ltd, 10 Alcorn Avenue, Toronto, Ontario, Canada M4V 3B2

First published in the United States of America by Dutton Children's Books,
a division of Penguin Putnam Books for Young Readers, 2001
Published by Puffin Books, a division of Penguin Young Readers Group, 2004

16 18 20 19 17 15

LIBRARY OF CONGRESS CATALOGING-IN-PUBLICATION DATA IS AVAILABLE UPON REQUEST.

Puffin Books ISBN 978-0-14-240124-8

Printed in the United States of America

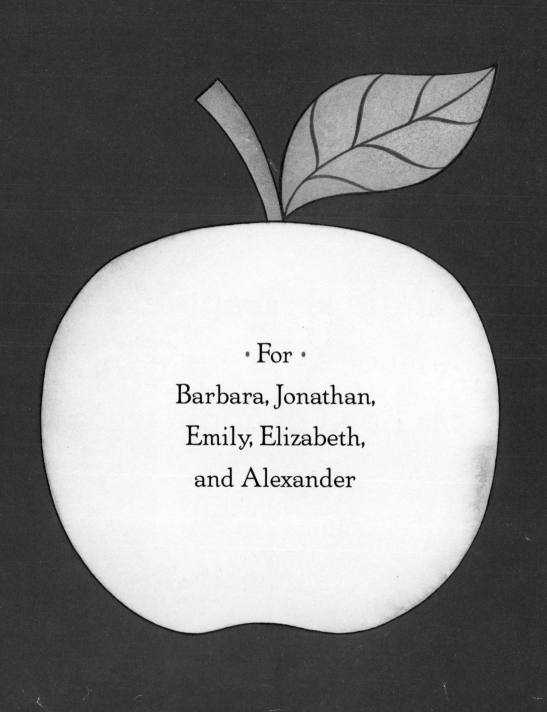

· For ·

Barbara, Jonathan,

Emily, Elizabeth,

and Alexander

Annie is an apple farmer. She has a big orchard of apple trees.

In the fall, she picks
baskets and baskets
of round, ripe apples.

She grows many kinds
of apples. She sorts and
organizes them.

Annie uses some
of the apples to make
sweet apple cider.

She uses others to make delicious smooth applesauce.

She loves baking muffins, cakes, and pies with her apples.

But she saves the
most beautiful
ones of all to sell
fresh at the market.

She loads everything
into her truck and
drives to the city.

Annie the apple farmer sets up her stand in the farmers' market.

Lots of customers come to Annie's stand. She is busy all day long.

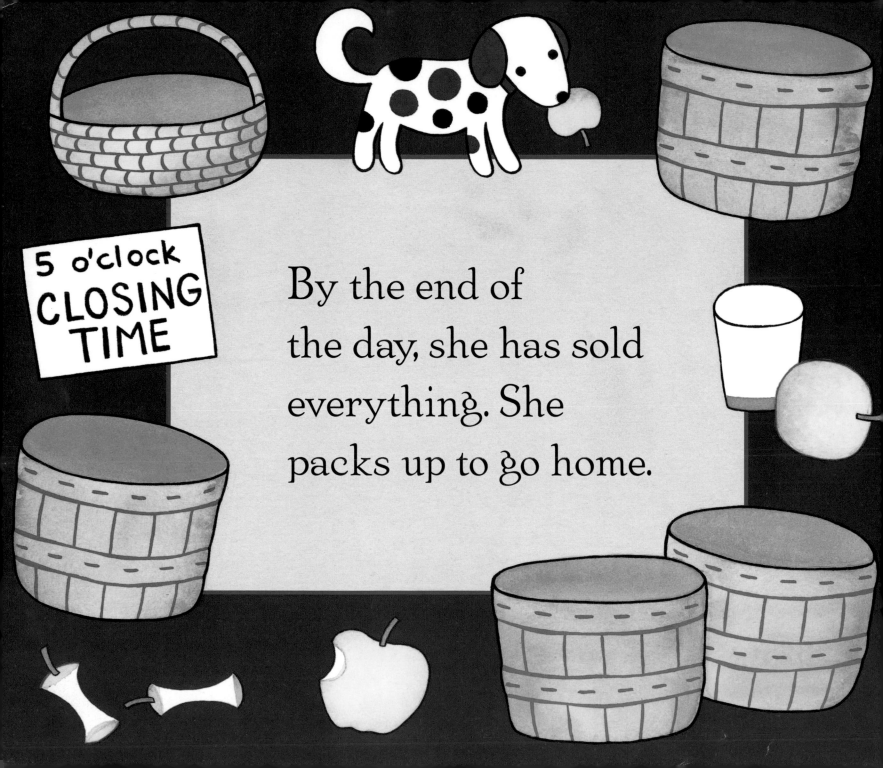

5 o'clock
CLOSING
TIME

By the end of
the day, she has sold
everything. She
packs up to go home.

Annie is tired but happy. It feels so good to have her own apple farm.

MY APPLE RECIPES

The BIG APPLE

Apple Varieties:
Baldwin
Cortland
Delicious
Empire
Granny Smith
Jonathan

Macoun
McIntosh
Northern Spy
Rome Beauty
An apple a day keeps the doctor away.

Applesauce

4 medium apples
¹/₂ cup water
¹/₄ cup sugar
   (approximate)
¹/₂ teaspoon cinnamon

Wash, peel, core, and slice 4 medium apples. Heat apples and ¹/₂ cup water to boiling, then reduce heat. Cover and cook slowly until tender and soft. Add sugar to taste (about ¹/₄ cup). Continue cooking until sugar dissolves. For extra flavor, add about ¹/₂ teaspoon cinnamon. For a finer applesauce, pour the cooked mixture through a strainer or sieve.

Apple Muffins

¹/₂ cup sugar
¹/₄ cup butter
1 egg
1 cup milk
2 cups flour
¹/₂ teaspoon salt
2 teaspoons baking
   powder
1 teaspoon cinnamon

¹/₂ teaspoon allspice
¹/₂ teaspoon nutmeg
   (optional)
1¹/₂ cups peeled,
   chopped apples

Topping
¹/₄ cup brown sugar
1 teaspoon cinnamon

Cream together sugar and butter. Add egg and beat well. Stir in milk. In another bowl, combine flour, salt, baking powder, and spices. Add egg mixture to flour mixture and blend until just moistened. (Batter will be lumpy.) Add apples to batter and blend carefully. Fill well-greased muffin tin. Sprinkle with sugar-and-cinnamon topping. Bake at 400 degrees for 20–25 minutes, until golden brown. Makes 1 dozen muffins.

Applesauce Cake

1/2 cup butter
1 cup sugar
2 eggs
1 1/4 cups flour
1/2 teaspoon baking
   soda
1/2 teaspoon salt

1 teaspoon cinnamon
1/2 teaspoon nutmeg
   (optional)
1/2 teaspoon allspice
   (optional)
1 cup applesauce
2/3 cup raisins

Butter Frosting

2 tablespoons softened
   butter
2 cups confectioners'
   sugar
1 teaspoon vanilla extract
3 tablespoons milk

Cream together butter and sugar in a large mixing bowl. Add eggs and beat well. In a separate bowl, sift together flour, baking soda, salt, and spices. Add to creamed mixture alternately with applesauce, beating after each addition and blending well. Stir in raisins. Pour batter into 9-inch greased tube pan. Bake at 375 degrees for 45 minutes or until browned. (Toothpick inserted into cake should come out clean.) Cool, then spread with Butter Frosting.

Cream together butter, sugar, and vanilla extract. Add milk and stir well. The frosting should be smooth and easy to spread.